THIS BOOK BELONGS TO:

Skates

Mick Inkpen

Red Wagon Books
Harcourt, Inc.

San Diego   New York   London

Tiger had some brand-new skates.

"They're Rollerblades," said Tiger. "Much better than ordinary skates, Kipper. Look, the wheels are all in a line!"

Tiger was not very good on his new skates. He kept wobbling and falling.

Then he rolled off down the slope, waving his arms and shouting, "Get out of the way!"

He crashed into Pig, who was walking with Arnold in the park.

Tiger struggled to his feet, and then fell over again.

"I haven't got any skates," said Pig. "Can I try yours?"

"No," said Tiger. "No, I wouldn't want you to hurt yourself. No."

So Kipper let Pig try his skates instead.

Pig was a terrible skater. He couldn't even stand up!

"What you need is practice," said Tiger. He was so busy telling Pig how to do it, he didn't notice he was rolling down the slope again.

He crashed into a bush.

"Ow!" shouted Tiger.
He had hurt his thumb.
"Ow! Ow! Ow!" He wasn't
very brave.

Kipper took him home for
a Band-Aid. Tiger wanted some
ointment, a sling, and some
candy, too!

"Let's go and show Pig my
bandage!" he said.

When they arrived at Pig's house, Pig and Arnold were in the garden. Pig was still wearing Kipper's skates.

"I want to show you something!" said Pig. He put on some music and began to skate.

"Wow!" said Kipper and
Tiger together.
Pig had been practicing.
He was brilliant!

And Arnold wasn't bad, either.

www.harcourt.com

Illustrated by Stuart Trotter

Library of Congress Cataloging-in-Publication Data
Inkpen, Mick.
Skates/Mick Inkpen.
p.   cm.—(Little Kippers)
"Red Wagon Books."
Summary: Even with his new in-line skates Tiger is a terrible skater,
but Kipper is good and, with a little practice, so is Pig.
[1. In-line skating—Fiction.   2. Roller skating—Fiction.   3. Animals—Fiction.]   I. Title.
PZ7.I564Sk   2001
[E]—dc21   2001002057
ISBN 0-15-216247-X
A C E G H F D B
Printed in Hong Kong